Mrs. Jeepers' Batty Vacation

There are more books about the Bailey School Kids!
Have you read these adventures?

Mrs. Jeepers' Batty Vacation

by Debbie Dadey
and
Marcia Thornton Jones

illustrated by John Steven Gurney

A
LITTLE APPLE
PAPERBACK

SCHOLASTIC INC.
New York Toronto London Auckland Sydney

To John Steven Gurney—a million thanks!

—MTJ and DD

ISBN 0-590-21244-3

Text copyright © 1997 by Marcia Thornton Jones and Debra S. Dadey. All rights reserved. Published by Scholastic Inc. LITTLE APPLE PAPERBACKS is a trademark of Scholastic Inc. THE ADVENTURES OF THE BAILEY SCHOOL KIDS in design is a registered trademark of Scholastic Inc.

10 9 8 7 6 5 4 3 2 1   7 8 9/9 0 1/0 2/0

Printed in the U.S.A.   40

First Scholastic printing, June 1997

Book design by Laurie Williams

Contents

1

Weirdest Vampire of All

"I have terrible news," Howie said to his friends Liza and Melody. They were gathered under the oak tree before the last day of school.

Eddie jumped out from behind the oak tree and looked at his friend. "Did you lose your mind?"

"Ha, ha," Howie said. "If I weren't so mad about this summer I might even think you were funny."

"What are you talking about?" Eddie asked. "We're going to goof off all summer. It'll be great!"

Melody nodded. "We can play soccer every day."

"We're going to relax. Mrs. Jeepers made us work hard this year," Liza said.

"After having a vampire teacher for

third grade, we deserve a great vacation," Eddie agreed. Most of the kids in their class thought Mrs. Jeepers, their teacher, was a vampire. After all, the brooch she wore every day did seem to have magical powers. Whenever anyone misbehaved, the brooch glowed and everyone shaped up.

"We can't be sure Mrs. Jeepers really is a vampire," Melody said.

"I know she is," Eddie said. "I saw the coffin in her basement. No one lives in a haunted house and has a magical brooch without being some kind of monster."

Howie sighed. "It doesn't matter, anyway."

Liza put her hand on Howie's shoulder. "What's wrong? You look like someone just gave you homework for the summer."

Howie sighed. "They did. My dad says I have to go with him on a scientific study."

"Yuck!" Eddie said. "That's cruel. How can your dad expect you to give up your summer to study science?"

Howie smiled. "I won't be studying science. He's the scientist. I'm just going with him. He thinks the trip will be very educational for me."

"There are plenty of educational things to do in Bailey City," Liza said.

"If you leave, then who will we play with all summer?" Eddie argued.

"You'll have Liza and Melody," Howie said. "I won't have anybody but my dad."

"Bummer," Eddie said, kicking the green grass under the oak tree.

"It doesn't seem fair," Liza agreed.

Melody twisted her pigtail and smiled. "Maybe we could talk to your dad and get him to change his mind."

"I don't think it would work," Howie said. "My dad wants me to get some culture on this trip."

"There's culture in Bailey City," Liza said.

Eddie rolled his eyes. "The only Bailey City culture worth getting is Doodlegum Shakes."

"Forget about Doodlegum Shakes," Melody told them. "Here comes Howie's dad."

"I'll get him to change his mind," Eddie said and ran toward Howie's dad.

"Don't get me in trouble," Howie called after Eddie.

But Eddie didn't stop. He ran up to Howie's father with Melody, Howie, and Liza right behind him. "Dr. Jones," Eddie said. "I don't mean to be rude, but I've got a question to ask you."

Dr. Jones pushed his glasses up further on his nose and smiled at Eddie. "What seems to be the trouble?" Dr. Jones asked.

"Howie belongs with his friends this summer," Eddie said. "Don't you want your son to be happy?"

Dr. Jones nodded. "I want that very

much," he said. "As a matter of fact, I agree with Eddie."

"You do?" Liza, Melody, Eddie, and Howie all said together. Hardly any grown-ups ever agreed with Eddie.

"That's why I've asked your parents if you kids can join us on our trip to Romania," Dr. Jones said. "My company offered to pick up the tab."

Howie's face lit up like a fireworks display. "You mean Liza, Melody, and Eddie get to go with us?"

"That's exactly what I mean," Dr. Jones said.

"All right!" Eddie yelled as Liza and Melody jumped up and down. Howie gave his dad a hug.

"That's not all of the good news," Dr. Jones said.

"There's more?" Howie asked.

"I've spoken with your teacher," Dr. Jones told them.

The four kids gulped when Dr. Jones

mentioned their vampire teacher. "Mrs. Jeepers?" Howie asked.

"Yes," Dr. Jones told them. "Mrs. Jeepers is from Romania. Her family still lives in the Transylvanian Alps, where we'll be staying. She is going home for a visit and has agreed to show us around."

"Mrs. Jeepers is going, too?" Howie asked, his face turning pale.

"Yes," Dr. Jones said. "I knew you'd be pleased. You've had such an exciting year with her as your teacher. Well, I've got to go now. I'll see you all on Monday for the trip."

No one said a word as Dr. Jones walked to his car and drove away.

"Oh, my gosh," Liza said. "We're going to Transylvania, the home of the vampires."

Eddie sat down on the ground with a thump. "And the weirdest vampire of them all is going to be our tour guide!"

2

Bloodsucking

Eddie shoved past his three friends to get to row thirteen. "I get to sit by the window," he said.

Melody, Liza, and Howie hurried to sit next to Eddie. They stuffed their Bailey School backpacks under the seats in front of them and buckled their seat belts. Howie's dad found his seat right behind Howie. All four friends turned and started talking to Dr. Jones at the same time.

"Will we get to see a movie?" Melody said.

"Can we have all the soda we want?" Eddie asked.

"I'd like some peanuts," Liza added.

"How long will it take to get there?" Howie asked.

Suddenly, Mrs. Jeepers towered over the four kids. She smiled an odd little half smile and gently touched the green brooch she always wore at her throat. The four friends stopped talking at once. "The plane trip to my home will take all evening," she said. "Night is the best time to travel."

Howie's dad leaned over the seats to talk to Liza, Melody, Eddie, and Howie. "We're so lucky to have Mrs. Jeepers along with us. She'll know all the ups and downs of traveling in Romania."

"Most bats are good at ups and downs," Eddie said under his breath.

Howie's dad continued to talk. "Mrs. Jeepers will be a great tour guide and can give you a real taste of the Transylvanian Alps."

Melody swallowed. "I just hope we don't become a tasty treat for Transylvanian vampires," she whispered to Liza.

Liza patted Melody on the arm. "We

have nothing to worry about," she said. "Howie's dad will be with us the whole time."

But then Howie's dad grinned. "Mrs. Jeepers has agreed to show you around while I work. She's even going to take you to her family reunion."

Mrs. Jeepers smiled back at Dr. Jones. Neither of them noticed the worried looks on the faces of the four kids. "My family cannot wait to have my students at the reunion. That will be a real treat."

"A reunion?" Eddie squeaked.

Mrs. Jeepers patted Eddie on the head. "Yes, my brother Boris, my mother, and several of my dearest old uncles and cousins will be thrilled to have you visit."

"I thought your family had to leave Transylvania," Howie said, remembering something his teacher told them long ago.

"Thankfully, most of my family has been able to return to our homeland."

Mrs. Jeepers smiled her odd little half smile again and sat down.

Eddie gulped, turned around, and ducked down in his seat. He grabbed Howie's arm and pulled him close. "Did you hear that?" Eddie whispered. "Mrs. Jeepers said we're a treat. Her family is going to spread us on their toast like jelly."

"Maybe we can still get off the plane," Howie said nervously. "Let's tell my dad we're sick."

Just then the plane engines roared to life, the plane raced down the runway, and soon climbed high above the clouds. Eddie tugged on Howie's shirt. Howie, Liza, and Melody leaned close to listen to what Eddie had to say.

"Mrs. Jeepers didn't get us during the school year, so now she's going to have her family do us in," Eddie told his friends. "We're going to a get-together of monsters. We're doomed."

"I knew it," Melody said. "We're going to be the main course at a vampire reunion."

"Shhh," Howie warned. "Mrs. Jeepers will hear you."

Liza nodded. "Besides, we never proved Mrs. Jeepers was a vampire. I'm sure her family is very nice. I bet Mrs. Jeepers eats hot dogs and plays badminton at her family reunion just like we do."

"Have you seen her eat hot dogs?" Eddie asked.

"No," Liza admitted.

"Have you ever seen her eat anything?" Melody asked.

"No," Liza told her. "But that doesn't mean a thing."

"It means we're in trouble," Eddie told his friends.

"It means you're batty," Liza said. "Stop all this crazy talk — you're scaring me."

"Be careful," Melody told her friends.

"You know when Liza gets upset, her nose sometimes bleeds."

Eddie gasped. "Melody's right. We can't let Mrs. Jeepers see blood. Whatever you do, Liza, don't let your nose drip blood . . . or it may be the last thing you do."

Liza's eyes got wide and Melody patted Liza's arm. "We need to calm down," Melody said. "All this talk of vampires is making us nervous." Just then, a hand reached out and squeezed Melody's shoulders.

"*AHHHHH!*" she screamed. Liza and Howie ducked, and Eddie covered his throat with his hands.

"I'm sorry," a sweet voice said. "I didn't mean to startle you." Melody looked up into the smiling face of the flight attendant.

Nobody said anything until the flight attendant finished putting trays of spaghetti and drinks in front of them.

Soon they were too busy slurping noodles to talk.

When they were almost finished, Melody tapped Liza on the shoulder. "I have to go to the bathroom," Melody said.

"Can't you wait?" Liza asked.

Melody shook her head. Liza sighed and got up to let Melody out. When Melody came back from the bathroom and slid back into her seat, she looked ready to cry.

"What's wrong?" Howie asked Melody. "Are you getting airsick?"

Melody shook her head. "I just saw Mrs. Jeepers' dinner, and you'll never believe what it was."

"Spaghetti," Eddie said. "That's what everyone is eating."

"Not Mrs. Jeepers," Melody said.

"What are you talking about?" Howie asked. But Eddie didn't wait for her answer. He kneeled in his seat and peered over the back. What he saw made him gasp.

He fell back in his seat and grabbed Howie's shoulder. "Melody is right. Mrs. Jeepers isn't eating. She's sucking blood out of a glass!"

3

Rough Ride

The plane was as dark as a bat's cave when Eddie and Howie woke up. Liza and Melody still slept peacefully. The only sound was the humming of the plane's engines.

"I don't care what Liza said," Eddie whispered to Howie. "Mrs. Jeepers' drink didn't look like tomato juice to me. It looked like blood."

"Mrs. Jeepers is probably asleep now," Howie said softly. "Why don't you look at her glass again?"

Eddie nodded and peered over the back of his seat. In a second he was sitting back down again, ghostly pale.

"What's wrong?" Howie asked. "Is Mrs. Jeepers awake?"

"Of course," Eddie said. "She's a vam-

pire and vampires don't sleep at night. She's still sucking blood. She must be on her eighth glass!"

"Maybe we should say something to the flight attendant," Howie said.

"I haven't seen her in a long time," Eddie said. "I bet Mrs. Jeepers sucked all her blood and now the flight attendant's lying like a lump of putty in the back of the plane."

"We have to do something," Howie said, "before she gets to the pilot, too."

Eddie nodded. "You have to tell your dad."

"He'll know what to do," Howie agreed. He took a deep breath and slowly looked over his seat. But Howie's dad didn't see him. Dr. Jones didn't see anything. He was slumped in his seat with his eyes closed tight.

Howie glanced at Mrs. Jeepers. Her eyes were wide open and she smiled her odd little half smile. Howie gulped and tried to smile back. Then he slid back down in his seat.

"What's wrong?" Eddie asked.

"I hope my dad's just asleep," Howie whispered with a trembling voice. "Or else Mrs. Jeepers already got him."

"You have to wake him up," Eddie said.

"It's too late," Howie gasped as the plane bounced and jiggled. "Mrs. Jeepers got the pilot, too."

Liza woke up with a start and screamed, "Oh, no! We're going to die!"

Melody opened her eyes and put her hands over her neck.

"Who is going to be next?" Howie said.

Mrs. Jeepers reached over and grabbed Liza's arm.

"Yikes!" Eddie gasped. "Mrs. Jeepers is going to suck Liza's blood!"

"Do not worry," Mrs. Jeepers told Liza. "The plane is just preparing to land. We are now in Romania."

As the plane descended, Liza, Howie, Melody, and Eddie peered out the window. Perched on the side of a mountain, a huge castle loomed in the distance.

"That looks like something out of a movie," Melody said.

"Yeah," Eddie muttered under his breath, "a horror movie."

"That," Mrs. Jeepers said with a smile, "is my childhood home, Castle Hauntly."

"Castle Hauntly!" Melody shrieked. Just looking at the tall pointy turrets gave Melody the shivers.

"Yes," Mrs. Jeepers said. "It is lovely. My mother still lives there."

"You must be kidding," Liza said. "After all, we're flying right past it."

Mrs. Jeepers smiled. "There are no airports near my home. We will take a train to Castle Hauntly."

Howie's dad patted Howie on the head. "It'll be so exciting for you to visit a real castle! You and your friends are very lucky."

Mrs. Jeepers and Howie's dad busied

themselves gathering the baggage while Howie slumped back down in his seat.

Liza looked ready to cry. "I don't want to go to that creepy-looking castle. I want to go home."

"Don't be such a wet noodle," Eddie said. "How bad can visiting an old lady be?"

Howie looked out the plane window at the storm clouds brewing in the sky above them. "This isn't any ordinary lady. This is Grandma Dracula!"

4

Batty Vacation

An old taxi drove slowly through the early morning traffic to an inn. Squeezed inside were Melody, Howie, Dr. Jones, Liza, Eddie, and Mrs. Jeepers. Liza shuddered as soon as she saw the tall gray inn.

Mrs. Jeepers looked at Howie's father. "I will arrange for our train to Castle Hauntly while you get your room at the inn." A moment later Mrs. Jeepers disappeared into the crowded street.

"Are you sure you want to stay here?" Howie asked his father.

Howie's dad glanced up. An attic window was cracked and two shutters banged against the gray splintery wood of the old house. "This place is great," he said. "It has real character."

"That's not all it has," Eddie whispered and pointed. Three bats flapped out of the attic window and flew into the thick cloud of fog.

"I have a bad feeling that this is going to be a very batty vacation," Melody said.

Dr. Jones opened the door to the inn and led the kids inside. It was so dark, they had to squint. What they saw sent goose bumps crawling down their backs.

Silver cobwebs clung to the dusty stair railing. A single candle flickered on a counter. Melody thought she heard something scurrying near her feet. Howie's dad didn't notice. He walked up to the counter to ring the bell three times.

From a back room, they heard slow, scuffling footsteps. Closer and closer they came. A huge shadow appeared in the flickering candlelight. Howie hid behind his dad. Melody and Liza backed up to the door. Eddie got ready to run when a short man with a face full of wrinkles appeared in the doorway behind the counter.

"May I help you?" the man asked with an accent that reminded the kids of Mrs. Jeepers.

Dr. Jones smiled. "I need a room for a few days."

The old man looked past Howie's dad at the four kids.

"Will they be staying, too?" he asked.

Dr. Jones shook his head. "They get to play while I work," he said. "They'll be staying with their teacher at Castle Hauntly."

"CASTLE HAUNTLY!" the man gasped, taking a step away from Dr. Jones. "You're sending them there?"

"So you know the place?" Dr. Jones said. "Mrs. Jeepers is going to show them around while I work. I'm the only one that needs a room."

The man looked straight into Dr. Jones' eyes. "Are you *sure* you want to send them there?"

"Of course," Howie's dad said. "I wouldn't have it any other way."

The old man picked up a pen and wrote down Dr. Jones' name. The old man's hand shook so hard the letters looked like squiggly worms.

"Is your dad blind?" Eddie asked Howie.

"Didn't he see how that man acted

when he heard we were staying at Castle Hauntly?" Melody hissed.

Howie frowned. "I need to talk to my dad."

But just then, the door flew open and the damp wind sent a pile of dead leaves swirling at their feet. Mrs. Jeepers loomed in the doorway.

"Our train is leaving," she said. "We must hurry."

Howie's dad handed the kids their backpacks and hurried them out the door. "Remember," he told them, "I'll come to Castle Hauntly as soon as my work is done. Be good." The door to the inn closed with a thud, leaving the kids out in the street alone. Mrs. Jeepers was already hurrying down the sidewalk. The four kids rushed after her.

"Where is she taking us?" Liza panted as Mrs. Jeepers led them down some dark steps.

"It looks like we're going into a bat

cave," Eddie said. At the bottom of the steps Mrs. Jeepers made them rush to hop aboard a train. As soon as they sat down, the train started rolling.

It didn't take long to leave the city. They rolled past miles and miles of farmland. Eddie tried counting the number of cows he saw, but there were too many. Suddenly, the train squeaked to a stop.

"Why are we stopping here?" Liza asked. "I don't see the castle anywhere."

Mrs. Jeepers rubbed the brooch at her neck. "The train is picking up a very special passenger," she said. Just then, the train doors slid open and a woman climbed on board.

"I would like you to meet my cousin, Justine Hauntly," Mrs. Jeepers said as the train took off. The four kids stared at Mrs. Jeepers' cousin. What they saw made them gulp.

Finally, Liza spoke in a wavering voice. "It's very nice to meet you. I'm

Liza and these are my friends Howie, Eddie, and Melody."

"Welcome to Romania," Miss Hauntly said with a heavy accent. "I am sure you will never forget your visit here."

Eddie poked Howie in the ribs and whispered, "I think I'm seeing double." Eddie was right. The stranger looked exactly like Mrs. Jeepers.

"One Mrs. Jeepers is bad enough," Eddie groaned softly. "How will we ever survive two?"

"Spending a weekend in a castle filled with Mrs. Jeepers look-alikes is not my idea of a vacation," Howie agreed quietly.

Even though it was the middle of the day it seemed dark to the kids. Rain started to fall and a steamy fog swirled up around the train. "Doesn't the sun ever shine here?" Liza asked.

"Actually, it is often sunny," Mrs. Jeepers said. "But I like the darkness and the rain. After all, farmland needs rain."

Miss Hauntly nodded her head and her

long red hair fell down across her shoulders. "I find the fog very comfortable," she said.

Eddie shivered and looked back out the window. None of the kids said another word until they had left the train and Mrs. Jeepers was pushing them through the fog toward a long black station wagon.

"Is that what I think it is?" Liza whimpered.

"It can't be," Howie said, his voice shaking. "Whoever heard of a hearse for a taxi?"

"To the castle," Miss Hauntly told the driver as they climbed in. The car skidded on gravel as it pulled away from the train station. They passed three potato farms before turning onto a gravel road and entering a forest full of spruce trees. The road grew steep as the car bumped over deep ruts in the muddy road. The rain had stopped, but it was still cloudy.

"Someone should pave this road," Eddie muttered.

"Many roads in Romania are only gravel," Miss Hauntly told him.

Liza took a shaky breath. "All these bumps are making me carsick."

"We're almost there," Mrs. Jeepers said. "Maybe a little fresh air will help." Mrs. Jeepers flashed her green eyes at Liza and her fingers gently rubbed the brooch at her throat. The windows slowly rolled down. Melody held her breath and Howie closed his eyes. They were sure Mrs. Jeepers was ready to zap Liza into a green lizard.

But Liza smiled at Mrs. Jeepers. "I'll be okay," Liza said. "The air is already helping me feel better."

Mrs. Jeepers turned back to look out the front window and the four kids rode in silence. That's when they heard it.

The noise started out low. Then it grew louder and louder. The high-pitched howl of wolves in the forest made Liza and

Melody whimper. Eddie's face grew pale and Howie's eyes looked like round marbles.

"Did you hear that?" Howie whispered.

Melody nodded. "Wolves," she said.

"The woods around Castle Hauntly must be full of them," Eddie said.

The black car made a sharp turn and rolled to a stop. "We are home," Mrs. Jeepers said.

5

Jeepers Creepers

Castle Hauntly loomed in the thick gray mist. A wooden bridge stretched across a muddy moat of water and led to the huge door of the castle wall. Two tall turrets reached high over their heads and disappeared into the gray clouds.

The silent driver hurried to unload the Bailey School kids' backpacks. Then he climbed back into the hearse and sped away.

Mrs. Jeepers smiled at the four friends. "Come meet my mother," she said. Mrs. Jeepers and Miss Hauntly hurried across the bridge.

Eddie looked at Liza and Liza looked at Melody. Then they all looked at Howie.

"We can't go in there," Eddie said.

"It's bound to be haunted," Melody added.

"We either go in there," Howie said slowly, "or we walk all the way back to the inn."

"I want to go home," Liza said.

Melody and Eddie nodded. "I say we start walking to the inn," Eddie said. Just then the cry of a wolf pierced the silence of the woods. Another nearby wolf answered. And then a third wolf howled.

"We're surrounded!" Eddie yelled.

"RUN!" Melody screamed. Then they grabbed their backpacks and raced across the drawbridge to catch up with Mrs. Jeepers.

"Do not fear the wolves," she told them while they caught their breaths. "They are too afraid to bother us. You will be quite safe."

Miss Hauntly lifted the huge brass door knocker and let it fall with a loud thud. Nothing happened.

"Maybe she's playing bridge with a neighbor," Eddie suggested. "My grandmother likes to play cards."

"My mother does not visit with the neighbors," Mrs. Jeepers said.

"Maybe she's shopping at the supermarket," Liza said. "My mother always shops for groceries when she's having company."

"There is no need for my mother to go to the store for food," Mrs. Jeepers told them. "Her food comes to her."

Melody gulped and Liza whimpered. Howie looked at Eddie. "I think we should go back to the inn." Howie's voice squeaked when he said it.

"That is not necessary," Mrs. Jeepers told them. "My mother will be here in a moment."

In the distance, another wolf howled and the flutter of wings beat over their heads. Melody and Liza ducked, but Eddie looked up at the sky. "Look," he yelled. "A monster bat!"

41

His friends looked in time to see a huge bat fly over the castle wall.

Mrs. Jeepers saw it, too. She smiled her odd little half smile and said, "Do not be alarmed." Suddenly, they heard footsteps inside the castle.

Slowly, the old door creaked open. Melody, Liza, Howie, and Eddie found themselves staring up at a tall woman. Her long black gown swirled at her feet, and long flowing sleeves ended at the tips of her fingers. Her fingernails were painted bright green, just like Mrs. Jeepers'. But her hair wasn't red like their teacher's. It was as black as a bat's wings and it hung down to her waist. The strange woman smiled at her visitors. Melody couldn't help noticing that her lipstick was the color of blood.

"Please come in." The strange woman spoke in a deep, slow voice. "I have been expecting you."

"Mother!" Mrs. Jeepers cried. Mrs. Jeepers and Miss Hauntly rushed to hug

the tall woman while the four kids huddled at the door.

"Jeepers creepers," Eddie gulped. "I think we're in big trouble now."

"I thought you said she'd be a sweet little old lady," Melody hissed at Eddie.

"She doesn't look like any mother I know," Howie admitted.

"Mother," Mrs. Jeepers said, "these are my students. The ones I have told you about."

Mrs. Jeepers' mother smiled. "It is a pleasure to meet you," she said. "My name is Madame Hauntly. We are looking forward to having you for dinner at our family reunion."

And then Mrs. Jeepers' mother led the four kids deep into the darkness of Castle Hauntly.

6

Secret Passages

"It must be very exciting to live in a castle," Liza told Madame Hauntly.

"Yes," Madame Hauntly said, "I suppose it is. It is also very lonely. I do not get many visitors. That is why I'm delighted you have come for a visit. It is an extra treat that you will be here for our family reunion. But I am sure you are tired, so let me show you to your rooms."

Madame Hauntly pushed open a huge wooden door and the four kids stared into a large room filled with tapestries and bloodred velvet curtains. Fat candles rested on gold candelabras in every corner of the room. The candles were already lit, casting eerie, flickering shadows throughout the room.

"Please rest and make yourselves feel

at home while I show these gentlemen to their room," Madame Hauntly told Liza and Melody. "We will eat later." With a thud, Madame Hauntly closed Liza and Melody in their musty-smelling room.

"What an unusual place," Liza said.

"Do you think they have cable?" Melody said with a giggle. "Or a heated swimming pool?"

"You could jump in the moat and swim a few laps," Liza suggested.

"But we'd have to dodge moat monsters," Melody said. The two girls laughed.

"I suppose we should rest like Madame Hauntly suggested," Liza said.

The girls pulled back the velvet covers on the enormous bed. They had barely lain down and closed their eyes when they heard a strange scraping sound. "What's that?" Liza asked, grabbing Melody's arm.

Melody popped open her eyes just in

time to see a portion of the stone wall move. "Whatever it is, it's coming to get us!" Melody squealed.

Liza looked ready to faint, but Melody didn't give her the chance. She pulled Liza out of bed and pushed a pillow into her hands. "Here, we'll bop whatever it is with these," Melody suggested.

Liza nodded as the wall scraped again. The opening got larger and larger. Scrape. Scrape. Liza gasped as a hand appeared through the opening.

"Yee-haw!" Melody said. Melody and Liza attacked the hand with their pillows.

"Ow!" Eddie said as his head appeared from behind the stone wall. "What are you trying to do — bop me to death with a feather pillow?"

"Eddie!" Melody shrieked. "What are you doing behind our wall?"

Eddie smiled. "Howie and I are exploring this secret passage."

Liza tapped her foot and folded her arms. "We're supposed to be resting."

"This is more fun," Eddie told them.

"It's dangerous," Melody said. "You could get lost."

Howie popped his head through the opening. "No, we're making sure we mark the way with these Rollie Pollies." Howie held up a box of Rollie Pollies candy.

"You shouldn't be sneaking around someone else's house," Liza told them.

"Madame Hauntly said we should

make ourselves feel at home," Eddie reminded her. "If I had a secret passage at my house, I would explore it. Besides, we're only going until we run out of Rollie Pollies."

"You can come, too," Howie told the girls as he and Eddie disappeared into the passage.

"We shouldn't," Liza told Melody.

Melody nodded. "I know, but I want to." Melody followed the boys.

Liza took one look around the candlelit castle bedroom. Shadows danced on the old stone walls. "Wait for me," Liza squealed. She grabbed something from her backpack, took a deep breath, and disappeared into the passage.

7

Bat Land

Liza expected to find a dark, damp hallway. Instead, the passageway was brightly lit by electric lamps that looked like candles. "Doesn't it seem strange that a secret passageway would be lit up like this?" Liza asked.

"Maybe it's not such a secret," Melody suggested.

"Maybe someone uses it a lot," Howie said.

Eddie looked at the dusty cobwebs hanging from the passageway ceiling. "Yeah, like a whole family of vampires on their afternoons off from biting the neighbors."

"Oh, Eddie," Liza said. "Madame Hauntly is very nice. Why, I bet she's even a grandmother."

"That's a horrible thought," Eddie told her. "Who'd want lots of little baby vampires running around the castle? They'd be biting anything that moves. It's a good thing my aunt Mathilda's dog isn't here. They'd drain his blood dry in a second."

"Eddie, there are no vampires here," Liza said.

"Look," Melody pointed, "that looks like a door."

"Don't open it," Liza said. "You don't know what's there."

"I thought you said there weren't any vampires here," Eddie said. "If that's true, then you have nothing to worry about."

Howie, Melody, and Eddie pushed on the heavy stone door. It creaked and scratched against the stone floor.

Scrape. Scrape. The door inched open. "Shhh," Liza said. "I hear something." The four kids paused to hear a strange fluttering sound.

"What is that weird noise?" Howie asked.

"There's one way to find out," Eddie told him. "Push." Melody, Howie, and Eddie pushed with all their might. The door popped open and the three kids fell into a completely dark room.

"There's something wet on the floor," Melody said. "It's all over my hands."

"I can't see a thing," Howie said, staring into the pitch-black.

"Here," Liza told them. "This will help." Liza reached into her pocket and pulled out a small travel flashlight. She shone it into the room.

"Oh, my gosh!" Liza squealed. "The room is alive!"

The four kids looked up to see what was making the fluttering sound. Hundreds of bats hung from the ceiling. A few bats were opening and closing their wings.

"If those are bats," Melody said, look-

ing at the wet sticky stuff on her hands, "then this must be . . ."

"Bat poop!" Eddie finished for her.

"I think I'm going to be sick," Melody said.

"Don't do it now," Howie suggested, "because I think the flashlight is waking up the bats."

The kids looked up to see all the bats flutter their wings. "Let's get out of here," Eddie exclaimed, "before Mrs. Jeepers' batty relatives decide to eat us for breakfast!"

The kids raced down the hallway with hundreds of bats chasing them.

8

Bat Poop

"We could have been eaten alive," Eddie told his friends the next day as they sat outside the castle.

"Bats don't eat people," Liza reminded him.

Melody covered her neck with her hands. "But vampire bats do suck blood," she said.

"You guys are full of bat poop," Liza said with a giggle.

"If you're so sure there aren't any vampires," Howie said, "why don't you go back in that passageway?"

Liza quickly shook her head. "No, thanks," she said. "That castle is too spooky. I barely got any sleep all night long."

"I kept expecting a bat to plop on my head," Howie agreed.

"At least it's not rainy today," Melody said, looking at the deep blue sky above the castle turrets.

"Too bad we don't have a soccer ball," Eddie said.

"Maybe we could walk around the castle," Liza suggested.

"Don't forget about the wolves," Melody said.

Eddie rolled his eyes. "The wolves are asleep. We'll just stay on the edge of the trees, anyway."

"Well," Melody said. "I guess that'll be all right."

"Yee-haw!" Eddie screamed and ran up to the nearest tree. He took a big jump and grabbed a low branch. In two minutes he was at the top of the tree. "Look at me!" Eddie shouted. "I'm a monkey man!" Eddie rubbed his hands under his armpits and grunted.

"You're going to be a dead monkey if you're not careful," Liza warned him.

"Look at that." Eddie pointed over the trees.

"What is it?" Howie asked.

"There's a little house right over that hill," Eddie told them. "Let's go see who lives there."

Liza shook her head. "I don't think that's such a good idea."

But Eddie didn't pay any attention. As he scrambled down out of the tree, his blue baseball hat fell off and landed on a branch. Without a word Eddie headed for the little house.

"You lost your cap," Liza told Eddie.

"That's okay," Eddie said. "I'll get it when we come back." The kids followed a twisting path through the tall trees. It led straight to the cottage.

"Isn't it cute?" Melody said when they finally arrived at the tiny cottage.

"It looks like the witch's house in

Hansel and Gretel," Howie said, "except that it's not made of candy."

"I think you're right," Eddie said, "because here comes the witch."

The four kids turned to see a tiny gray-haired woman rushing toward them. Her gray dress was worn and patched. She carried a shovel in her hands and a frown covered her face. She shouted something that the kids couldn't understand, except for the names Hauntly and Jeepers.

"Let's get out of here!" Melody squealed. "Before she buries us alive!"

The four kids ran screaming from the old woman. In two minutes, they were far away and totally lost. Huge spruce trees completely blocked out the blue sky and the kids found themselves in a dark, almost cavelike clearing.

"I don't like this," Liza said.

"Don't worry," Howie said. "I can get us out of here."

Eddie gulped. "Unless you have radar in your pocket, we're in deep bat doo."

"You had radar on your head," Howie said with a smile. He scrambled up a nearby tree and disappeared into the thick branches. His three friends waited and waited at the bottom of the tree.

"Is he all right up there?" Liza said.

"The question is," Melody whispered, "are we all right down here?" She pointed at a nearby bush. It was shaking and the kids heard a rustling sound.

"What is it?" Liza said, jumping behind

Melody and peering over her shoulder.

"Maybe it's more vampire bats," Eddie said. As soon as he'd said that, all three kids put their hands over their necks.

The bush shook again and a creature emerged. It had four legs and white spots.

"It's only a deer," Liza said with relief.

"A fawn," Melody corrected her, "a baby deer."

"I'm just glad it's not that old woman chasing us with her shovel," Eddie said.

"That was really strange," Liza admitted, still looking at the fawn. "Remember how she screamed out the names Hauntly and Jeepers?"

"Do you think she was trying to warn us about something?" Melody asked.

"Probably to get away from Castle Hauntly as fast as we can," Eddie said.

"The people we meet sure don't seem to like Castle Hauntly," Liza agreed.

"That's because they know something we don't know," Eddie said.

"Yeah," Melody agreed. "Like how to find our way out of this forest."

"No problem," Howie said from above them. He came crashing down and landed with a thump on the forest floor. The fawn skittered away as soon as Howie landed on the ground. "I know exactly how to find our way back."

Eddie crossed his arms. "How do you know that?" he asked.

Howie pointed to Eddie's red hair. "For once, you used your head — or rather your hat. Remember you left your baseball hat in the tree?"

His three friends nodded.

"All we have to do is follow the blue cap home," Howie said with a grin.

Melody patted Eddie on the back. "I'm glad to see you have something useful in that peabrain of yours."

"Besides," Howie added, "the castle's a little hard to miss when you're up in the tree."

"Let's go," Liza said. "I've had all the adventure I can stand for one day."

"Back to Castle Hauntly," Howie said, "and who knows what adventure waits for us there, because today the rest of Mrs. Jeepers' family arrives."

9

Boris

Eddie peeked inside the dingy hallway. "It's safe," he told his friends. "Follow me."

Eddie led Melody, Liza, and Howie deep inside Castle Hauntly. "Where are you taking us?" Liza asked.

"We should be going to the dining room," Howie said. "It's almost lunchtime."

Eddie stopped to face his friends. "The last place we should be is in the dining room."

"You don't really believe Mrs. Jeepers and her family are planning to eat us, do you?" Liza asked.

"It's the perfect way for a vampire teacher to get rid of her students," Eddie told her.

"He does have a point," Melody said. "And most teachers would do anything to get rid of Eddie."

Eddie pulled Melody's pigtail. "Very funny, bat-brains."

"Ouch," Melody squealed and bopped Eddie on the arm.

"Shhh," Liza warned, but she was too late. A tall dark figure appeared at the far end of the hall.

"Children," Madame Hauntly called. "My son is waiting to meet you. Please come in. I also want to introduce you to my other relatives."

"This is all your fault," Melody whispered to Eddie. "We could've sneaked away, but now we have to go in there."

"You're the one that screamed," Eddie snapped.

"Would you two stop fighting?" Howie interrupted. "We have to figure out how to stop from being the main course."

Eddie pulled up his shirt collar until it

reached his ears. "We'll have to get by Uncle Bloodsucker first," he said.

The four kids slowly walked to a door at the end of the hall. "Go ahead," Melody said.

"No," Eddie said. "You first."

"Both of you go," Howie said. He gave his friends a big push. Eddie and Melody fell into the room and bumped right into a very tall stranger.

"How nice to meet you," a deep voice said. "I have heard so much about you."

Melody and Eddie looked straight up into the face of a man with hair as red as Mrs. Jeepers'. His face was as white as milk and he wore a black cape buttoned at his throat. The button was red and reminded Melody of a big drop of blood.

The man smiled, showing two very long and very pointy eyeteeth. "My name is Boris Hauntly," he said. He shook Melody's hand and reached for Liza's hand. When he did, he licked his lips.

Madame Hauntly waved her hand toward the dining room. An entire room of tall, pale people smiled, showing long pointy eyeteeth. All those pointy teeth were too much for Liza. She took one look and shrieked. She turned, running from the room as fast as she could.

"Where is she going?" Mrs. Jeepers asked.

"I'll find out," Eddie said. Then he raced after Liza.

Melody looked at Howie and Howie looked at Melody. Then they both looked at Boris Hauntly. He smiled and licked his lips again.

"Let's go!" Melody yelled. Howie and Melody darted out of the room. They took the steps two at a time and caught up to Eddie and Liza at the top of a curving stairway.

"This is crazy," Howie panted.

"He's right," Melody said. "We can't outrun Mrs. Jeepers' batty family."

"We have to," Eddie said. "It's our only chance." The four kids nodded and took off running in different directions.

"This way," Eddie yelled to his friends.

Liza pointed to a different hall. "Our rooms are this way," she said.

"That's the first place they'll look for us," Melody told her and pointed down a third hallway. "This goes to the tower steps. We could hide there."

"Are you nuts?" Howie asked her. "The

tower would be a favorite napping place for all of Mrs. Jeepers' batty relatives."

"What are we going to do?" Liza wailed.

"Whatever it is, we'd better hurry," Eddie said. He pointed down the steps. There stood Boris Hauntly and the whole Hauntly family.

"Wait," Boris called. "Come back."

"He wants to suck our blood dry," Eddie squealed. "I'm not going back there."

"Follow me," Howie said. "I have a plan." They raced after Howie, leaving Boris behind. Howie dashed down one hall, turned right, and ran some more. At the end of that hallway, they sped to the left. Flickering lamps lit the dim hallway that dead-ended in front of a heavy wooden door.

"What do we do now?" Melody asked.

"We go through the door," Howie said.

Liza gulped. "I don't want to."

"It's either that," Eddie said slowly, "or go back the way we came."

"Where Boris Hauntly is waiting," Melody reminded him.

Liza took a deep breath. Then she nodded at the door. "Let's do it."

Melody grabbed the cold iron doorknob and pulled. As the door squeaked open, damp air whooshed out. Then Melody disappeared into the darkness.

10

Torture Chamber

Eddie, Liza, and Howie followed Melody down cold stone steps. The air grew colder the further they went. Finally, Melody stopped at the bottom.

"Where are we?" Eddie asked.

Melody turned and faced her friends. When she spoke, her voice shook. "We're trapped in a dungeon!"

Liza shook her head. "It's an ordinary basement like we have at home, only this one is wetter and older."

Howie pointed to a wall. "There's nothing ordinary about that," he said softly. On the wall, above Howie's head, were rows of chains with metal rings attached.

"That's strange-looking," Melody said. "What are they?"

Eddie raised his arms and looped them

through the rings. "These are what you call manacles," he told his friends. "Don't you know anything?"

"So I suppose you know what this is?" Liza said, pointing to a wooden tablelike contraption.

"That," Eddie said, rolling his eyes, "is a rack. It's for stretching people."

Melody giggled. "Maybe that's how Boris Hauntly got so tall."

Eddie took off his baseball cap and looked around the room. "Haven't you ever watched late-night TV?"

Melody, Liza, and Howie shook their heads. "My mom won't let me stay up that late," Melody admitted.

"Well, if you stayed up late once in a while you'd know where we are," Eddie told them.

"I think I'm beginning to figure it out," Howie said. "That rack isn't for stretching Boris. It's for stretching kids like us who give Boris trouble."

"You mean we're in a torture chamber?" Melody said.

"Yeah," Eddie said. "This was probably the Hauntly kids' playground. We had swing sets and the little vampires had a torture chamber."

"Don't talk like that," Liza said. "You're scaring me."

Melody gulped. "I have a feeling we have a reason to be scared. Listen."

Thump. Thump. Thump.

"What is that?" Howie asked.

"It's either a loony rabbit trapped in Castle Crazy or Boris coming down the steps," Eddie said.

The four friends looked at one another and shouted. "Boris!"

"We have to get out of here," Liza squealed.

Melody pulled open another door. "Let's see where this leads," she said.

The four kids went up and up on the

twisted steps. "I'm getting dizzy," Liza moaned.

"I feel like a yo-yo," Eddie complained. "First we were down, now we're going up."

"We can't stop now," Howie said. "I still hear Boris."

"What are we going to do if he catches us?" Melody said.

"We can't think about that now," Eddie said. "We've just got to keep going." Up and up they went. Finally, they could go no further.

"We're at the end of the road!" Liza yelled, pounding on the solid wall that stood in front of them.

"Maybe not," Howie said. He pounded on the wall beside Liza. Suddenly, the wall moved.

"It's another secret passage," Melody said. The four kids started pounding together. On the stairs below them they heard footsteps.

Thump. Thump. Thump.

"Hurry!" Eddie shouted. The four kids pounded and the wall moved slowly. It scraped open just as a large, pale hand grabbed Howie on the shoulder.

11

Anything for a Friend

"He's got me!" Howie screamed. "Do something!"

"Run!" Eddie shouted. He slid through the doorway and into the secret passage. Liza and Melody squeezed in behind him.

"I mean do something to help me!" Howie shouted after his disappearing friends.

Melody and Liza skidded to a stop, but Eddie kept running. "We can't leave Howie back there," Liza said.

"But we can't leave Eddie alone, either," Melody told her.

"I don't like this one bit." Liza sniffed, like she was getting ready to cry.

Melody grabbed her friend's arm.

"Don't cry, Liza. We have to be brave," Melody said.

Liza sniffed again. "I'll try," she said, but she didn't sound very sure.

"We have to figure out how to save Howie," Melody said.

"And Eddie," Liza added.

"I'm not worried about Eddie. Vampire bats probably find him as sour as teachers do. We'll go back for Howie first," Melody decided. "Then we'll find Eddie."

"What if Boris is waiting for us?" Liza asked. "How can two small third-graders from Bailey Elementary fight a seven-foot-tall vampire from Transylvania?"

"Good point," Melody said. "Is Howie worth fighting over?"

Liza stopped to think. "Friends are always worth fighting for," she finally said.

"You're right," Melody said. "I just hope we're not too late."

Together, Melody and Liza tiptoed toward the massive stone door. They

pressed their ears to the door and listened very carefully.

"I don't hear anything," Liza whispered.

"We have to go back through the door," Melody said. "Are you ready?"

Liza took a deep breath, then nodded. The two girls held hands and pushed through the giant door, ready to battle the evil Boris. But he wasn't there. Neither was Howie. The top of the twirling stairway was absolutely empty.

"Oh, no," Liza cried. "We're too late."

"Poor Howie," Melody said. "I bet Boris changed into a giant bat and swooped away with Howie."

"There's nothing more we can do for Howie," Liza said sadly. "We'd better go save Eddie."

Liza and Melody gave the empty chamber one last look. Then they squeezed back through the secret door and made their way up the passageway.

"My legs are tired from steps," Liza complained. "It feels like we're climbing all the way to the moon."

Melody nodded. "This must lead to the tower."

"I don't want to go to the tower," Liza said. "I want to go home."

"Me too," Melody said, "and we will as soon as we find Eddie."

A chilly gust of wind whipped down the curving stairs and made Liza shiver. "I think we're almost to the top," she said through chattering teeth.

"I hope Eddie's waiting for us," Melody said. "Maybe then we can work on finding Howie."

"If there's anything left to find," Liza said hoarsely. Together, the girls climbed the last stair and stepped into a tower room. What they saw almost made them faint.

Eddie was there and so was a very big bat. Between the bat's pointy little ears was a patch of bright red fur. Eddie

stared at the bat. The bat stared right
back at him.

"Is that who I think it is?" Melody
whispered, pointing to the bat.

Eddie spoke through clenched teeth.
"It's Boris, all right," Eddie said. "And he
has us cornered!"

12

Damsels in Distress

"We're not vampire cookies, yet," Melody said. She rushed to the edge of the tower and leaned over the edge. "Help!" she called. "Help!"

"Oh, my gosh," Eddie said. "The rest of the family is already here!" A long dark shadow from the stairway loomed over the three kids.

"I think I'm going to faint," Liza said.

Eddie clenched his fists, ready to fight. "They're not taking us without a fight. We'll save ourselves and then we'll go back for Howie."

Melody nodded and positioned herself in a karate stance. Liza gulped and grabbed a loose rock from the tower floor.

"I can see the headlines in the Bailey City paper," Liza moaned. "'Four students creamed in Transylvania, details on page four.'"

"My mom will cry her eyes out," Melody said.

"No, she won't," Eddie said, "because we're not going to die."

Just then the huge shadow stepped into the tower, along with a smaller shadow. "Help!" Liza screamed and closed her eyes. "There are two of them!"

Melody patted Liza on the shoulder. "Is it over?" Liza gasped. "Am I dead yet?"

Eddie laughed. "Not yet, dingbat," he said. "Open your eyes and see."

Liza opened her eyes. There stood Howie and his father. Liza gave Howie a big hug. "I'm so glad to see you," Liza said. "We thought you were bat cream pie."

Howie smiled. "Me too. But it was my dad. He came to do some sightseeing with us."

"I think I've seen all of Transylvania that I want to see," Melody said.

"Oh, no," said a deep voice. "Your adventures have only begun."

The four kids and Dr. Jones turned to stare into the green eyes of Boris Hauntly.

"Yikes!" Liza squealed and jumped behind Melody.

"If Boris is here, then who's that?" Eddie asked. The four kids turned around to look at the big bat.

"It's gone," Melody said with a gulp.

"Boris tells me you children ran off," Dr. Jones said. "Is anything wrong?"

Eddie and Melody shook their heads. Liza spoke softly, "I'm sorry I ran. It was rather rude of me. I just got scared."

Boris leaned his head back and laughed. When he did his big eyeteeth showed. "Scared of me?" Boris said. "My sister will tell you that I'm as gentle as a lamb."

Mrs. Jeepers stepped up behind Boris and patted him on the shoulder. "Boris is gentle, as long as he does not get hungry. Then, watch out."

Liza, Melody, Howie, and Eddie stepped back from Boris. "I hope you're not hungry now," Melody said.

"As a matter of fact," Boris said, reaching for Eddie, "I'm starved."

13

News

"This is delicious," Boris Hauntly said, smacking his lips and licking his fingers.

"Yes, this is a fine meal," Miss Hauntly said. She smiled at Mrs. Jeepers and Boris.

Liza squirmed in the ancient chair and tried not to look at Mrs. Jeepers' family and the large platters of strange-looking food spread out before her and her friends. Boris and Mrs. Jeepers had taken everyone into the huge dining hall for dinner. Liza had been afraid Boris was going to eat Eddie, but instead Boris was munching on a large piece of round black bread that he dipped in some kind of red sauce.

Across the table from Liza sat Mrs. Jeepers and Miss Hauntly sharing a big

platter of cheese. They dipped every bite of cheese in the strange red sauce.

Madame Hauntly was seated at the head of the table in a huge wooden chair that looked like a throne. She nodded as a servant carried in a big platter filled with pies the size of large pizzas.

"Hey, this is good!" Howie said, taking a great big bite of potatoes.

A tiny gray-haired lady nodded as she placed another enormous platter of red meat on the table. She was the same woman they had seen outside the castle. She was no longer in an old gray dress. Now she wore a starched white cook's outfit.

The tiny woman said something to the Bailey School kids, but they couldn't understand a single word she said.

"My cook says thank you," Madame Hauntly translated for them.

The cook smiled at the kids and started talking again.

"She tried to warn you not to get lost in the woods," Madame Hauntly said. "But you only ran away."

"We did get lost," Melody admitted, "but just for a minute."

Madame Hauntly smiled. "She did not realize you only speak English. We are all glad you returned safely. Now, please eat. She cooked a special meal just for you."

"I'm not eating anything if I don't know what it is," Eddie said, crossing his arms over his chest. "For all I know, this stuff could be turtle eyeballs."

"No," the old woman said. "I made no eyeballs today. Try some garlic noodles."

Eddie grimaced and took a small helping of the noodles. "Yum, these taste almost as good as a Doodlegum Shake." Eddie gulped down his noodles and went back for seconds.

Liza noticed that none of Mrs. Jeepers' family touched the noodle bowl, but they ate lots of the red meat. Boris chose the reddest-looking piece to bite.

Madame Hauntly smiled at Liza. "We are so pleased to have you visit our home. Please eat."

"Thank you," Liza said politely. She took a small chunk of brown bread and passed the plate to Dr. Jones.

"This looks great. Thank you," he said.

Madame Hauntly stood up from the table and looked at her family and friends. "We have so enjoyed our visitors from America. It is time we should return the favor."

"What are you saying?" Mrs. Jeepers asked her mother.

"Dear daughter," Madame Hauntly said. "I would be pleased to visit America and our new friends."

Boris stood up and raised his glass. "I also have an announcement."

"Oh, no," Melody said to Liza. "Maybe Boris is still planning on eating us."

Boris continued. "I would like to make a toast to America. I have heard wonderful things about it. I want to hear more. That is why I followed you earlier. When Mother goes to America, I shall accompany her. Perhaps I will even stay and live there."

"Holy moly," Eddie said. "You mean you're moving to Bailey City?"

Boris nodded his head. "I am certainly thinking about it. I hope I can even talk Mother and a few more relatives into joining me."

Miss Hauntly held up her glass. "Good luck to you, Boris. We will miss you."

"Uh-oh," Melody whispered while the Hauntly family toasted Boris. "Do you think America is ready for Mrs. Jeepers' family?"

Liza shook her head. "I'm sure Bailey City isn't ready for them," she said softly.

"Pass me some more garlic noodles," Eddie said.

Mrs. Jeepers frowned at Eddie. "Please remember to close your mouth when eating."

"Sorry," Eddie said, showing a mouth full of noodles. He reached for the noodle bowl and knocked over his glass. Milk splashed everywhere. Mrs. Jeepers, the cook, and Miss Hauntly rushed to clean up the mess.

"The question is," Liza said with a giggle, "is Transylvania ready for Eddie?"

Four short days later, the kids and Dr. Jones boarded the airplane to head back to Bailey City. Mrs. Jeepers and her entire family came to see them off.

"Thanks for the wonderful tour of your homeland," Dr. Jones told Mrs. Jeepers.

"It was my pleasure," Mrs. Jeepers said. "I will be back in Bailey City in another week. Hopefully, my family will also join me."

"Children," Dr. Jones said, "don't forget to thank Madame Hauntly for her hospitality."

Liza piped up, "Thank you for letting us stay at your castle."

"Thank you," Melody and Howie said together.

"It was an experience I'll never forget," Eddie admitted. Mrs. Jeepers and her family waved as the four kids and Dr. Jones boarded the plane.

"Whew," Eddie said as soon as they sat down on the plane. "I'm glad I'm out of that nest of bloodsuckers."

"It wasn't so bad," Liza said. "It was even kind of neat staying in a castle."

"What are you talking about?" Melody asked her. "Remember running off screaming when Boris smiled at you?"

Liza's face turned red as the plane roared off the runway. "I guess I over-reacted a little bit."

"Only because you thought Boris and the Hauntly family might drain us dry," Howie reminded her.

"They still might," Melody said. "Don't

forget they're coming to visit Bailey City, maybe even to live there."

Liza shook her head. "Once we get back in Bailey City, I'll feel perfectly safe. After all, we'll be home. And there's no place like home."

"Except," Eddie said, "when your home is a place like Bailey City!"

Hauntly
Gallery

Take a close look at these portraits hanging in Castle Hauntly. Can you find the bats hidden in the pictures?

❧ 2 BATS ❧

Batty Activities
and Puzzles

A Batty Maze

Can you help Mrs. Jeepers find her way home?

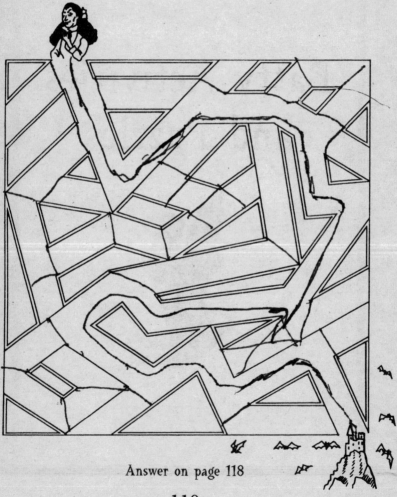

Answer on page 118

A Batty Word Search

Find the words in the haunted castle below. Words can be horizontal, vertical, diagonal, and even backward!

VACATION · AIRPLANE · TRANSYLVANIA
MRS. JEEPERS · HAUNTLY · CASTLE
SPOOKY · BATS · CREEPY · VAMPIRE

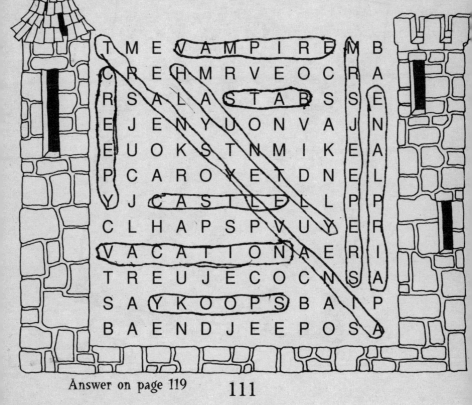

T M E V A M P I R E M B
C R E H M R V E O C R A
R S A L A S T A B S S E
E J E N Y U O N V A J N
E U O K S T N M I K E A
P C A R O X E T D N E L
Y J C A S T L E L L P P
C L H A P S P V U Y E R
V A C A T I O N A E R I
T R E U J E C O C N S A
S A Y K O O P S B A I P
B A E N D J E E P O S A

Batty License Plate Game

Using letters on road signs, you can try to spell words. Try spelling your name or your favorite food! The first person who spells a word wins! (You have to make sure that someone else in the car sees the letters!)

A Batty Sing Down

You don't have to be a great singer to play this game. You just need to remember the words to your favorite songs.

Here's how you play: One person thinks of a word, for example let's say *yellow*. Now everyone must think of songs with the word *yellow* in the song. Take turns and see how many songs you and your friends can sing. Then change the word! You can make teams, too!

We're Going on a Picnic

You and a friend (or as many people as you want) can plan an excellent picnic! Each player has to think of something to bring and remember what everyone has said before! The players must use the alphabet as a guide. It will help you remember things, too!

Howie: I'm going on a picnic and I'm going to bring an **A**pe.

Liza: I'm going on a picnic and I'm going to bring an **A**pe and a **B**anana split.

Melody: I'm going on a picnic and I'm going to bring an **A**pe and a **B**anana split and a **C**hocolate-chip cookie.

Eddie: I'm going on a picnic and I'm going to bring an **A**pe and a **B**anana split and a **C**hocolate-chip cookie and a **D**oodlegum Shake!

(Keep going until you get to the letter Z. Can you remember all the things?)

A Snack for the Journey

Monster Trail Mix

You will need:
raisins
nuts (peanuts or sunflower seeds)
chocolate chips or chocolate candies

Pour all of the ingredients into a bowl
and mix. It tastes good and will give
you lots of energy on your trip!

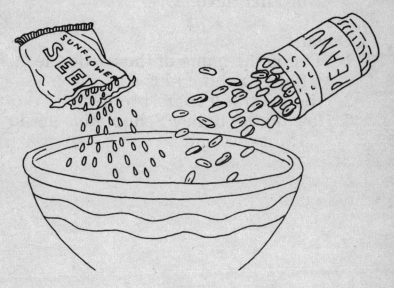

A Batty Crossword Puzzle

Now that you've read *Mrs. Jeepers' Batty Vacation*, can you fill out the answers to this puzzle?

Across
1. Whose Dad takes the Bailey School kids to Transylvania?
2. What is in the secret passage at the castle?
3. What color hair does Mrs. Jeepers' mother have?
4. What color hair does Mrs. Jeepers' brother have?

Down
1. What is the name of the castle the Bailey School kids stay in?
2. Who is Mrs. Jeepers' brother?
5. How do the Bailey School kids get to Transylvania?

Answer on page 119

117

Puzzle Answers

Hauntly Gallery
pg. 106

Hauntly Gallery
pg. 107

Hauntly Gallery
pg. 108

A Batty Maze
pg. 110

Puzzle Answers

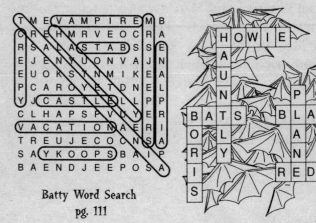

Batty Word Search
pg. 111

A Batty Crossword Puzzle
pg. 117

119

Debbie Dadey and Marcia Thornton Jones have fun writing stories together. When they both worked at an elementary school in Lexington, Kentucky, Debbie was the school librarian and Marcia was a teacher. During their lunch break in the school cafeteria, they came up with the idea for the Bailey School Kids.

Recently Debbie and her family moved to Aurora, Illinois. Marcia and her husband still live in Kentucky where she continues to teach. How do these authors still write together? They talk on the phone and use computers and fax machines!